# Fur and Feathers

by Janet Halfmann

illustrated by Laurie Allen Klein

The howling wind wakes Sophia. Her mother suggests that they count animals to help them forget about the noisy storm.

They count together: one polar bear, two ducks, three snakes . . . and then Sophia is sound asleep.

But in her dreams, the animals whirl with the whipping wind. Faster and faster they spin, till the wind blows them right out of their coats. Fur, shells, feathers, and scales fly everywhere. The animals shiver in their bare skin.

"Don't worry," says Sophia. "I'll help you stay warm."

From her closet, she grabs every piece of clothing she owns. *Push! Pull! Tug!* She helps the animals fit tails, fins, and wings into her kid-sized outfits.

The animals are thankful . . . but they find it hard to walk, crawl, or fly. And they think they look terribly silly!

Sophia can tell by their expressions that the animals are not happy. But what can she do? Then she remembers her grandma's huge sewing box, bulging with furs, feathers, and sequins.

"I can make new coats for all of you, just like your old ones," she exclaims. "Form a line and tell me what you need."

Polar Bear pads forward first. "I need a coat of thick, white fur to keep me warm and to help me hide in the ice and snow," she says.

*Snip, tuck, stitch.* In no time, Sophia fashions a furry new coat for Polar Bear. Behind one ear, she sews a little red heart. But Polar Bear doesn't notice.

Duck waddles up next. "I need lots of feathers to help me fly," he quacks.

Sophia pulls a big bag of feathers from Grandma's sewing box. Duck helps her find the right colors. Soon, he has gray body feathers and glossy green head feathers. But the white ring he once wore around his neck is now bright blue—Sophia's favorite color.

Then it's Porcupine's turn. "I feel lost without my prickly quills," she grunts. "How am I going to protect myself?"

Sophia hunts through Grandma's sewing box for something sharp, when suddenly *OUCH*—she pricks her finger on a pin.

"That's it," she says, "pins and needles."

A few finger pricks later, Porcupine has a new brown fur coat bristling with pins and needles.

Frog hops up. "I don't wear a coat over my skin," he croaks, "but the wind whisked away my covering of slime. I need it to stay moist. Do you have any slime in there?"

Sophia checks, but there's no slime. Everyone thinks and thinks about what to do. But Frog can't think without hopping. Higher and higher he jumps . . . till his big eyes spy a tub of green slime on a toy shelf.

Sophia pours the slime all over Frog, letting it ooze from head to toe. Happily slimed, Frog hops away into the night.

"Can I be next so I can get back to the water?" calls Fish from the back of the line. Everyone steps aside to let her go ahead.

"I need smooth scales so I can *swish, swish, swish, lickety-split,*" she says. "And please slime me, too."

Sophia chooses sequins for Fish. All decked out in slimy, shiny sequins, Fish is not only the fastest, but the flashiest!

"I wear scales, too," hisses Snake, "but I need dry ones."

"*Hmmmm*, let's try these pinecone scales," says Sophia. Using light and dark ones, she creates a beautiful spotted pattern of overlapping scales. As a special touch, she adds a few bright yellow bows.

Snake smiles when he sees the bows, and slithers proudly away.

Now, Sophia hears a wee voice coming from far below. She bends down to listen.

"I need a shell to keep me safe and moist," whispers Snail.

Sophia rummages through Grandma's button box and finds a pretty, striped shell for Snail.

Then another small voice pipes up. "The wind blew off my colorful wing covers," says Ladybug. "Now I can't warn birds that I taste awful."

Sophia cuts tiny new wing covers out of red plastic. On them she draws little black dots—and two stars.

Ladybug opens her new wing covers and extends her flying wings, happy to be a *STAR*!

All night long, Sophia sews new coats for an endless parade of animals—and adds her own special touches.

In the morning when she wakes up, her mother has a surprise. The whole family is going to spend the day at the zoo.

"Look," exclaims Grandma, pointing to a polar bear. "That bear has a red heart behind her ear!" Sophia just smiles.

# For Creative Minds

## Scientific Classification

Just as we sort money or candy, scientists sort all living things into groups to help us understand and connect how things relate to each other. Scientists ask questions to help them sort or classify animals.

Based on the answers to the questions, scientists can sort the living organisms. The first sort is into a Kingdom. There are five commonly accepted Kingdoms: Monera, Protista, Fungi, Plantae, and Animalia. All of the living things in this book belong to Animalia or the Animal Kingdom.

The next big sort is into a Phylum. One of the first questions that a scientist will ask is whether the animal has (or had at some point in its life) a backbone. If the answer is "yes," the animal is a vertebrate. If the answer is "no," the animal is an invertebrate.

Each Phylum is broken down into Classes, like mammals, birds, reptiles, fish, insects, or gastropods (snails). Then each class can be broken down even further into orders, families, genus and species, getting more specific.

The scientific name is generally in Latin or Greek and is the living thing's genus and species. People all over the world use the scientific names, no matter what language they speak. Most living organisms also have a common name that we use in our own language.

### Questions scientists ask:

Does it have a backbone?

What type of skin covering does it have?

Does it have a skeleton? If so, is it inside (endoskeleton) or outside (exoskeleton) of the body?

How many body parts does the animal have?

Does it get oxygen from the air through lungs or from the water through gills?

Are the babies born alive or do they hatch from eggs?

Does the baby drink milk from its mother?

Is it warm-blooded (endothermic: maintains a nearly constant body temperature), or cold-blooded (ectothermic: uses the heat of the sun or surrounding water to warm itself)?

# Mammals:

hair, fur, whiskers, or quills at some point during their lives

backbone (vertebrate)

inside skeleton (endoskeleton)

lungs to breathe

most give birth to live young

produce milk to feed young

warm-blooded

# Birds:

feathers

backbone (vertebrate)

inside skeleton (endoskeleton)

lungs to breathe

hatch from eggs

warm-blooded

# Fish:

most have scales covered with a thin layer of slime

backbone (vertebrate)

inside skeleton (endoskeleton)

gills to breathe

babies are either born alive or hatch from eggs

cold-blooded

# Amphibians:

soft, moist skin

backbone (vertebrate)

inside skeleton (endoskeleton)

most hatchlings are called larvae or tadpoles and live in water, using gills to breathe

as they grow, they develop legs and lungs and move onto land

cold-blooded

# Reptiles:

dry scales or plates

backbone (vertebrate)

inside skeleton (endoskeleton); most turtles also have a hard outer shell

lungs to breathe

most hatch from leathery eggs

cold-blooded

# Insects:

hard outer covering

no backbone (invertebrate)

outside skeleton (exoskeleton)

adults have 3 body parts: head, thorax & abdomen

most hatch from eggs

cold-blooded

# Gastropods (Snails):

most have hard shells

no backbone (invertebrate)

outside skeleton (exoskeleton)

hatch from eggs

cold-blooded

Kingdom  Phylum  Class  Order

Family  Genus  Species

# Skin Coverings

## Hair (Mammals):

comes in different colors or patterns

helps some animals camouflage

helps protect the skin

helps animals to stay warm

can be:
thin (like on our arms or legs)
thick fur
whiskers
eyelashes
quills

## Hard Casing (Adult Insects):

protects body

wings attach to casing

sheds (molts) as animal grows

bright colors may warn of poison

some colors camouflage

## Dry Scales or Plates (Reptiles):

protect the animal while crawling
on the ground

waterproof to keep the animal's
skin from drying out

snakes and skinks have
overlapping scales

turtles have hard outer shells
that grow with them (the scales
on the shells are called scutes)

snakes shed (molt) their skin all
at once as they grow

other reptiles shed (molt) their
scaly skin in chunks as they grow

## Feathers (Birds):

come in different shapes, sizes, and colors

help keep birds warm (insulate)

are used to fly

are used for camouflage

are used to attract female's attention

are kept clean by preening

four different types of feathers:
long, stiff feathers for flight
tail feathers for balance and steering
short, soft under-feathers for warmth
longer feathers to smooth things out

## Wet Scales (Fish):

scales overlap from head to tail
for easy swimming

some scales are big and can be
removed one by one, but some
are so tiny they are barely visible

a slimy mucus over the scales
helps protect the fish

## Shells (Snails):

shells are bones found on the outside of an
animal's body (exoskeleton)

just as our bones grow with us, the shells
grow with the animals

the hard shells protect the soft bodies

## Soft, Moist Skin (Amphibians):

protects animals

adult skin secretes a slime (often
poisonous as protection)

adult amphibians breathe oxygen
through their skin

# Animal Classification

Use the information found in the book to match the animal to its classification.
Answers are upside down.

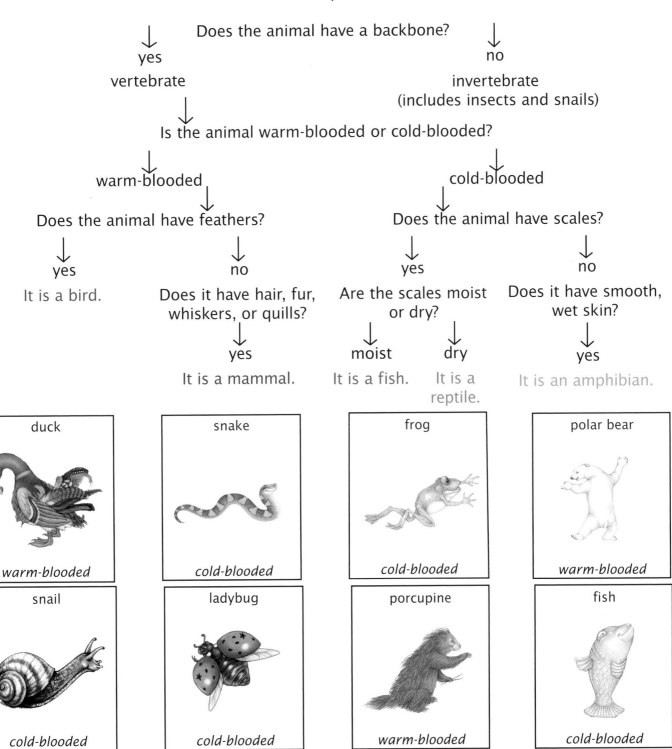

Does the animal have a backbone?

↓ yes
vertebrate

↓ no
invertebrate
(includes insects and snails)

↓
Is the animal warm-blooded or cold-blooded?

↓ warm-blooded

↓ cold-blooded

Does the animal have feathers?

↓ yes
It is a bird.

↓ no
Does it have hair, fur, whiskers, or quills?
↓ yes
It is a mammal.

Does the animal have scales?

↓ yes
Are the scales moist or dry?
↓ moist
It is a fish.
↓ dry
It is a reptile.

↓ no
Does it have smooth, wet skin?
↓ yes
It is an amphibian.

duck
*warm-blooded*

snake
*cold-blooded*

frog
*cold-blooded*

polar bear
*warm-blooded*

snail
*cold-blooded*

ladybug
*cold-blooded*

porcupine
*warm-blooded*

fish
*cold-blooded*

With love to my grandkids, great-nieces, and great-nephews—JH

All my thanks to my mom for her sewing inspiration, to Rafi S. for posing, to my friends for their constant encouragement, and forever to Bob & Jesse—my heart and inspiration—LAK

Thanks to Loran Wlodarski, Educator at SeaWorld Orlando, for verifying the accuracy of the information in this book.

Publisher's Cataloging-In-Publication Data

Halfmann, Janet.
Fur and feathers / by Janet Halfmann ; illustrated by Laurie Allen Klein.

p. : col. ill. ;  cm.

Summary: A story of a young girl who dreams that howling winds whisk fur and feathers right off her animal friends. Trying to help, she sews each of them a new "coat." But what kind do they need? Who needs fur, and what color? Who needs feathers, and why? Who needs scales, and should they be moist or dry? Includes "For Creative Minds" educational section.

ISBN: 978-1-60718-075-3 (hardcover)
ISBN: 978-1-60718-086-9 (paperback)
Also available as eBooks featuring auto-flip, auto-read, 3D-page-curling, and selectable English and Spanish text and audio
Interest level: 004-009
Grade level: P-4
ATOS™ Level: 3.4
Lexile Level: 750 Lexile Code: AD

1. Animals--Classification--Juvenile fiction.  2. Adaptation (Biology)--Juvenile fiction.  3. Animals--Classification--Fiction.  4. Adaptation (Biology)--Fiction.  I. Klein, Laurie Allen.  II. Title.

PZ10.3.H136 Fu 2010
[Fic]          2010921907

Manufactured in the USA
This product conforms to CPSIA 2008

Arbordale Publishing
formerly Sylvan Dell Publishing
Mt. Pleasant, SC 2946
www.ArbordalePublishing.com